Laura Lee Gulledge

AMULET BOOKS

NEW YORK

But I'm not totally alone, because I moved here with my parents.

They're writers. Hence my name is Paige Turner. A name destined to write acclaimed books. Or something.

Oh, and we also brought along Harley. Best. Cat. Ever.

But I don't feel totally like myself around them. I bite my tongue a lot. It just makes things easier...

But when I close my eyes, I'm more like THIS under the surface: I'm laughing and screaming and scheming and daydreaming.

Living quietly feels safer. But artists draw inspiration from challenges, right? What have I learned from playing it safe?

And I hate how all my friends now live in picture frames.

Without them, I'll just have to rely on myself. And this sketchbook. And some pencils. And a LOT of erasers.

I am a redheaded island.

Where to start? Well, according to Grandma, the only thing you have control over as an artist is HOW MUCH art you make. Don't worry about the path; just go.

So I'll do a few pages each week, focusing on one drawing at a time. Page by page...or rather, page by Paige.

Okay,
just draw.

Something.

ANYTHING!!

I must be making this too hard.
I should draw what I know.
But what do I know?

So I went out for inspiration...

New city.

New Paige.

Rule #3

Shhh... quiet...
listen to what's going
on in your head.

-January-

The inside of my head
is a loud place.

I tell myself that everyone else feels alone, too.

I feel like I'm swirling down the drain...

Hey Red! What's your IM name? Wanna chat online? =-) --Jules

Or maybe I just worry too much.

Now my head is swirling in a different way... with ideas.

What is it that I don't like about myself?

1. I don't ask for help. I'm stubborn and get frustrated easily.

2. I've always been such a late bloomer. I feel awkward, behind, sheltered.

...and move some wires around.

It's funny how risks on paper spill over into real life. Facing fears in my 2-D world helps me in my 3-D world.

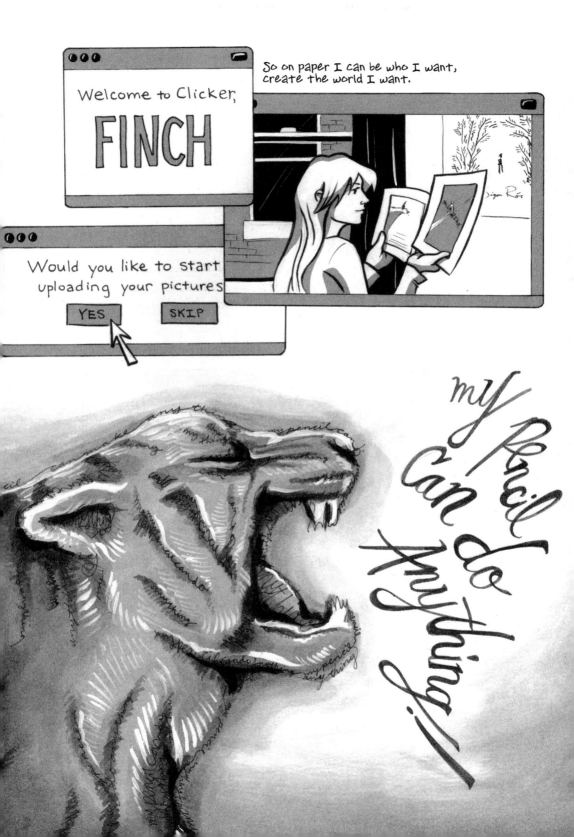

Welcome to Clicker, **FINCH**

So on paper I can be who I want, create the world I want.

Would you like to start uploading your pictures

YES   SKIP

my Pencil can do Anything!

It's like a weight has been lifted, a costume has been shed.

Bad experiences are like bad drawings. They stay in our sketchbooks. They stay a part of us. You can't erase your past or who you are. You have to deal with it, I suppose.

If my drawings speak on my behalf, then what do they say? It's not the real me. I'm selling a lie.

I always do this. I make things more complicated than they really are.

The more I think,
the more tangled up I get...
ARRRGGG!!!!!

And I didn't draw for a week.

I think I was born with my eyes facing the wrong way.
Because they're always looking back into my head rather than looking out.

If I can tap into something inside me, then I should...right?? I shouldn't apologize.

To art or not to art? I have an idea who else understands this dilemma...

Paige: Hi! :-)

 Longo: Hey there, Turner!

 Paige: Hey, you used to draw a lot, right?

 Longo: Yeah, I used to be quite the cartoonist.

 Paige: Soooo why don't you draw anymore?

 Paige: And don't give me that "stuff came up" crap.

 Longo: Okay, fine! So last year I applied to a special summer program thing being taught by one of my IDOLS.

 Longo: I went in with my drawings, and he said I needed way more practice. My stuff was undeveloped. To try back next year. Etc.

 Longo: I was CRUSHED because I was SO SURE I would get in. After that I decided to take a break from drawing, and I just have not gotten around to drawing anything since then.

 Paige: That's terrible! :-(But it's been a long time. Why don't you try to get back into it?

Longo: I dunno, the longer I wait the harder it becomes. The pressure builds up. It's just easier to leave it in the past.

Paige: But do you miss it?

 Longo: Yes.

Paige: What are you doing after school tomorrow?

(Support)

(This is a drawing Longo and I made TOGETHER!)

My heart didn't even write a farewell note...It was a goner.

I'm trying to let myself feel things instead of avoiding them...

...but there is so much going on at any given moment.

But then the next minute I'm overwhelmed with the bad stuff... like social anxiety.

In fourth period we had a sub, so Longo and I made some drawings together. It made me think of Diana, since we used to do the same thing back in Virginia.

And then we all played a game of Drawing Telephone. How do you play? Well...

n person needs pencil paper. You can use a ck of loose sheets or gle sheet folded up.

Write a sentence. Any sentence! Pass it to the next person.

Next person reads the sentence, folds it back, and in the next section illustrates it.

Pass it. Look at the drawing, fold it back, and write a sentence of what you think it is.

Pass it. Next person illustrates the new sentence. And so on, and so on...

Reading Gabe's story felt strange, like I was invading his privacy somehow. I decided to copy down part of it here... I hope he doesn't mind.

"...but our story didn't start 'Once upon a time...,'" the boy objected.

"Did, too." The old man sniffed. "But we didn't hear it, because we're lucky enough right now to be the tale, not he who tells it."

"Well, who's telling it?" the boy asked, looking around as though he expected to see a storyteller nearby.

"Maybe you, one day, to another young mind. Maybe another teller of tales readin' this, not knowin' they're in the middle of their own story."

"I still don't get why stories are important," said the boy. "What's wrong with leaving happenings just being stuff that, y'know, happened?"

The old man clicked his tongue and said, "Now that is a right-thinkin' question! I'll tell you why: Tellin' stories makes us impossible."

The boy threw his hands up in the air in exasperation. He'd thought he'd been on the edge of understanding the old man, but now he was once again adrift in seeming contradictions.

"Take Mister Flutterbye, if you need an example," said the old man, extending a finger like a gnarled branch. To the boy's amazement, a butterfly came to rest on the offered perch.

"Mister Flutterbye, to your eyes, is just a bug, ain't he?" The old man didn't wait for confirmation. "But for all you know, he could have a wife and kids back home, an' you pinchin' his wings there could have ended up deprivin' 'em of a husband an' a father, couldn't it? Unlikely, I know, but it all depends on the kind of story. As another for instance, while this little fella here is flappin' those wings of his, he could be causin' a hurricane on the other side of the world."

"Now you really are making things up."

"No I ain't. That's a kind of magic your little friend Tommy could take a lifetime and never understand, too. This world ain't about how big you are, or how little.

"It's about how every little thing touches every other thing in creation. But if you don't like that, how about we look at you?"

"Me?"

"Yup, you. Ain't nothin' in the world more impossible than a little boy."

"What do you mean?" The boy had never thought of himself as...well, as anything more complicated than a little boy.

"Little boys are like doors into the impossible. Like when you're playin' games. When you're playin' a game of make-believe, are you still you? Or are you a spy? Or a cowboy? Or a knight? Who are you when you're playin' those games? And what do you think you're doin' when you play those games? You're tellin' another story."

The old man waved his hand, dismissing the butterfly the way someone else would dismiss a misunderstanding. "It ain't even just when you're playin', either." He pointed his gnarled finger at the boy.

"Every little boy is his mother's little angel, and his father's reflection. And because all little boys are a little bit wild, they all have a bit of the jungle in 'em behind the eyes...every little boy is a tiger. An' every little boy is someone's shadow, and a hundred other things besides, because every little boy—heck, every child—is a door into the impossible."

"And what are you, then? Are you lots of things, too?"

The old man chuckled, and the boy felt a warm glow of pride in his chest; he was only favored with that laugh when he had impressed the old man with his understanding.

"Old men ain't nothin' except old men. Old men is what you kids become when you've stopped being everything else. An' I'll tell you somethin', my boy, bein' an old man is the one thing you don't get to choose..."

I like the idea that people are made up of different things...so I wondered what would make up Gabe.

Gabe Recipe

To make one Gabe you will need:

* Six feet of organic-grown, grade-A, fair-trade, FDA-approved sincerity
* Two cups of mixed notes, theories, and quiet observations
* Three heaping spoonfuls of X-ray vision
* One fresh heart, still on the sleeve
* Two tablespoons of Paige fluency

Blend together all the above ingredients in a tub of Play-Doh, then dispense through a Fun Factory.

Garnish with prose and shenanigans to taste.

Play-Doh

I ♥ VAMPIRES

They're nice to visit, but not all of them are for me.

I've been playing in the same dollhouse my whole life, and I've only just NOW started adding new rooms, exploring new scenes and subcultures. Jules calls this "reality surfing."

Indie Nerds

Street Punks

Hipsters

Goths

Com... Ner...

Musicians

NO I AM BEING IRONIC

Hippie...

Steampunk & DIY

Bike Kids

Being a "Girlfriend"

Street Artists

But so many distractions do make it hard to sit still and draw about it.

I have GO in me!

This is yet another thing I inherited from my mom, who also has trouble sitting still.

Some people help the world
by planting real trees...
I plant drawn ones.

In my mind, we live up to our feathery code names. We won't apologize for being birds!

*Wookie noise

And what is my gut telling me now?
To take the plunge and trust myself.

It's time to find
out if I can swim...

It's up to me to grow
my own beanstalk if I
want to climb anywhere.

Acknowledgments

Special thanks to: My lovely family for always encouraging me to draw, for your support, and for your trust as my ideas grew perpetually (and foolishly/bravely) bigger. All my Charlottesville and New York friends for knowing when to drag me away from my desk...and for knowing how to inspire me to go back. Jason Longo, Jamie Rodger, Geoff Sprung, and Alex Dezden for contributing your words and drawings on behalf of my characters. Diana Arge, Bishop 203, Matt Mikas, Julie Bissell, and Christian Larson for your game of Drawing Telephone. Maya Rock, Dan Lazar, Maggie Lehrman, Chad W. Beckerman, and the folks at Abrams for taking a chance on me and my difficult-to-categorize artwork.

About the Author

Laura Lee Gulledge, like Paige, grew up in Virginia and moved to New York. Also like Paige, she started sharing her personal drawings online in order to try to better understand herself and her adopted city. She has worked in art education and scenic painting, among other pursuits. This is her first graphic novel. She currently lives in Brooklyn, New York. Visit her online at whoispaige.com.

Mix for Paige

Page by Paige Soundtrack

(Selected musicians who were referenced in the book)

Jules's Faves...

"Infinity Guitars" – Sleigh Bells
"Carpetbaggers" – Jenny Lewis
"Easy" – Joanna Newsom
"Better" – Regina Spektor
"Cheated Hearts" – Yeah Yeah Yeahs

Gabe's Faves...

"Hannah" – Freelance Whales
"Scythian Empires" – Andrew Bird
"Anthems for a 17-Year-Old Girl" – Broken Social Scene
"Pavement Tune" – The Frames
"All My Friends" – LCD Soundsystem
"This Year" – The Mountain Goats
"Exo-Politics" – Muse

Longo's Faves...

"Animal" – Miike Snow
"I'll Be Better" – Francis and the Lights

Paige's Faves...

"I and Love and You" – The Avett Brothers
"Ragged Wood" – Fleet Foxes
"Dancing with Myself" – Nouvelle Vague
"The Clockwise Witness" – DeVotchKa
"40 Day Dream" – Edward Sharpe & the Magnetic Zeros
"Gobbledigook" – Sigur Rós

Laura Lee's musician friends
who have inspired and supported her...

"Golden Days" – The Damnwells
"Purple Weather Girl" – Samuel Stiles
"We Will Become Ourselves Reborn" – Ki:Theory
"Up Against Life" – Small Town Workers
"Gravity" – The Dirty Dishes
"Thankless" – All of Fifteen
"Rules of the Game" – Moneypenny
"Going Through Changes" – Army Of Me

For my mother, her mother,
and all quiet souls with
loud imaginations
—L.G.

Library of Congress Control Number: 2010930150
Hardcover ISBN: 978-0-8109-9721-9
Paperback ISBN: 978-0-8109-9722-6

Text and Illustrations copyright © 2011 Laura Lee Gulledge
Book design by Laura Lee Gulledge and Chad W. Beckerman

Additional material courtesy of Alex Dezden (pages 120, 137, 182), Jamie Rodger (pages 141-143), Matt Mikas (pages 135-136), Diana Arge (page 135), Julie Bissell (page 135), Bishop 203 (pages 135-136), Jason Longo (pages 118, 134-136, 173, 183), and Geoff Sprung (pages 68-69, 158, 176, 182-183).

Printed and bound in U.S.A.
10 9 8 7 6 5 4 3 2 1

Amulet Books are available at special discounts when purchased in quantity for premiums and promotions as well as fundraising or educational use. Special editions can also be created to specification. For details, contact specialmarkets@abramsbooks.com or the address below.

ABRAMS
THE ART OF BOOKS SINCE 1949
115 West 18th Street
New York, NY 10011
www.abramsbooks.com